Games and activities for 5-11 year olds

Welsh

It's Wales

Fun and Games

Ethne Jeffreys

y Lolfa

First impression: 2002
© Copyright Ethne Jeffreys and Y Lolfa Cyf., 2002

Cover design: Ceri Jones

ISBN: 0 86243 627 3

Printed on acid free and partly recycled paper
and published and bound in Wales by:
Y Lolfa Cyf., Talybont, Ceredigion SY24 5AP
e-mail ylolfa@ylolfa.com
internet www.ylolfa.com
phone +44 (0)1970 832 304
fax 832 782
isdn 832 813

Contents

Foreword

This book for leaders was published originally with a Swansea Citizenship Millennium Award, and I am grateful to both the Millennium Commission and the City and County of Swansea who enabled me to distribute 500 copies, free, to primary schools, public libraries and childcare groups in the County and beyond. My Millennium Project is completed but interest in the book has continued. To meet demand, it is now being published commercially.

The idea for the book came from Lucy Osborn, the manager of the after-school club at Pen-y-fro Primary School, Dunvant, Swansea (where I was a governor from 1992 to 2000), who alerted me to the dearth of traditional games books on the market.

Most of the games come from my experience as a child and later as a youth leader in the 'fifties and 'sixties. I have updated some and made up a few more, gleaning ideas from several people. Variations are suggested, and I'm sure the reader will think of others. Some games have been added from other sources which are acknowledged on p.108. As traditional games come to us from a less affluent age, few materials are needed – what are can usually be found in the home, school or club.

For easy reference I have categorized the games and activities, and in most cases indicated the number of players for which a game is suited. I have also suggested the age-group (index) to which each game might appeal. While this can only be a general guide, seeing that children develop differently, I hope it may be of help to leaders new to working with children.

I have recently tried out many of the games with local groups across the 5-11 age-range to see how today's children respond to them. Nearly all were given the 'thumbs up'; those that weren't were either changed in the light of suggestions by the children and their leaders, or axed. My thanks to them for their enthusiasm and readiness to take part in the project.

My wish is that these games will provide fun and put children in touch with part of their heritage. At the same time they could be one answer to current concern about lack of physical exercise leading to childhood obesity. I also hope the games will help children develop socially by interacting with others through play rather than 'relating' merely to the TV or computer screen.

While written with the after-school club in mind, the book may be used by teachers for playground games (and occasionally in the classroom), or by anyone caring for primary-age children. I hope, too, that children themselves may see it in a public library and dip into it.

Ethne Jeffreys
February 2002

CHASING GAMES

These games allow children to 'let off steam', and provide much-needed exercise while they have fun. The games could be suitable for school playtime or the start of a meeting when children can join in as they arrive.

The games need no equipment and may be played either indoors (space permitting) or outdoors (weather permitting).

Leaders should check that there are no hazards indoors (chairs, equipment lying around) or pitfalls outdoors such as holes in the ground, muddy patches or dog-mess. Outdoors, the play area should have well-defined boundaries and players should be within sight of leaders supervising the games.

COLOUR TOUCH
(large or small number)

1   One player is the Chaser, who says, "Touch colour…" (names a colour), and chases the others until they touch it.

2   If the Chaser touches anyone before she/he has touched the colour named, that person becomes the new Chaser.

Variation: Play simply as Touch, where the Chaser runs after the others and the one touched changes places with the Chaser.

FREEZE TOUCH
(large or small number)

1   One player is the Chaser, another the Rescuer.

2   When the Chaser touches anyone, that player has to 'freeze', holding out one hand.

3   The Rescuer runs around trying to 'melt' the frozen players by tapping them on their outstretched hands.

4   Game ends when all are 'frozen', including the Rescuer.

Variation: If game goes on too long, have more than one Chaser.

CROCODILE IN THE RIVER
(large or small number)

I   Chalk 'river banks' on floor if played indoors. (Outdoors: a safe, even spot to serve as a river.)

River bank

About 2 metres

River bank

2   Choose one player to be the Crocodile in the river:

3   Each time the leader says 'GO', the others run from one river bank to the other, trying not to get caught by the Crocodile.

4   Those who are caught join the Crocodile and help to catch others as they cross the river. (If players are slow to cross the river, leader gives them up to a count of 5 to cross – otherwise they're out.)

5   Last to be caught wins.

LONDON

(large or small number)

I   Players line up behind a starting point. (Could be a chalked line indoors or end of building outdoors.) Starter stands a few metres away from the others, back towards them.

Starting point

2   Starter spells out "L-O-N-D-O-N, LONDON" in a loud voice.

3   As Starter spells out the word, the others creep up on him/her.

4   After spelling out "London", Starter turns around. Everyone 'freezes'. If Starter sees anyone move, tells them to go back to starting point.

5   Game continues (steps 2-4). First one to touch the Starter without being seen becomes the new Starter.

Note: Players find it helpful to practise spelling out "London" before the game starts. For younger players (under 7 years), a card with "London" printed on it would be a good visual aid.

WHAT'S THE TIME, MR WOLF?

(large or small number)

I   Fix a starting point.

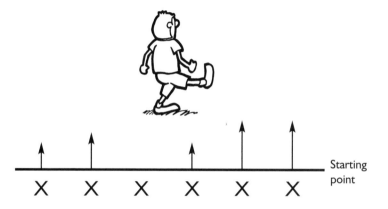

Starting point

2   Mr Wolf stands a few metres away from the others, back towards them, and starts walking.

3   Others follow, chanting, "What's the time, Mr Wolf?"

4   Mr Wolf turns around and tells them a time (e.g. "One o'clock"), then turns back and continues walking.

5   Others keep following him and chanting. Each time Mr Wolf turns around he gives a different time, BUT

6   when Mr Wolf cries "Dinner-time" he chases the others back to the starting point. If he catches anyone, that player becomes the next Mr Wolf.

RELEASE
(at least 5 players)

I   Choose a spot to be the Monster's Den – corner of a yard, or doorway, for instance. One player is the Monster who guards the den. Another player is a Slave who chases the others.

2   Once someone is caught the Slave takes him/her to the den where the Monster stands guard. The Slave then catches more prisoners.

3   However, those players who haven't been caught can RELEASE prisoners if they can touch them. (Prisoners stick their arms out of the den behind the Monster.)

4   Game ends when all the players are caught.

Variation: To bring the game to a quick end, or where there's a large number of players, more than one Slave may do the chasing.

CIRCLE GAMES

There's something harmonious about a circle: sitting, standing or joining hands in a ring promotes playing together. These games may be energetic, calming, or draw out the children's imagination. (SEE also Singing Games for circle play.)

CAT AND MOUSE
(at least 10 players)

1   Players form a circle. One is the Cat, who is outside the circle; another is the Mouse who is inside.

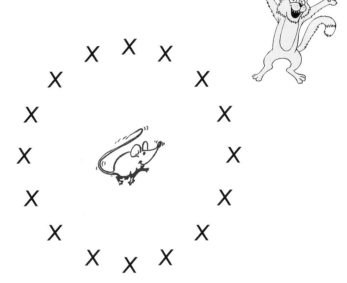

2   Cat tries to catch Mouse by getting into the circle through spaces between players.

3   Players squeeze up to close any gap.

4   If Cat gets inside the ring and touches the Mouse, the Mouse becomes the new Cat. Another player is chosen to be the Mouse.

CHINESE WHISPERS
(small groups)

1   Players sit in a circle of 6-7.
2   Leader whispers a short message to the next player (e.g. "Mothers' Day is next Sunday").
3   That player whispers the message to the next person, and so on till everyone in the ring has heard it.
4   The last person to hear it says what she/he THINKS the message is! (The result is usually very funny.)

Note: For large numbers, have players sitting in small circles. Best if leader starts the Chinese Whisper if undesirable messages are to be avoided!

I WENT TO MARKET
(small or large number)

1   Players sit in a circle. One starts, "I went to market and bought a _____ " (names something).
2   The next person says, "I went to market and bought a _____ (repeats what the previous player has bought) and a _____ " (adds something else).
3   The list of items is repeated by each player, who adds something to it.
4   If a player forgets an item, or gets one wrong, she/he is out.
5   Game continues until only the winner remains.

Variation: Use the letters of the alphabet to name purchases – e.g.

| 1st player: | "I went to market and bought some <u>a</u>pples." |
| Next player: | "I went to market and bought some apples and a <u>b</u>alloon." |

LAND, SEA OR AIR

1 Players are told the actions to be used:

Land	=	Walking action
Sea	=	Swimming action
Air	=	Flap arms

2 Players form a circle, with one of them (the Actor) in the middle.

3 The Actor stands in front of someone in the circle and does an action for Land, Sea or Air.

4 That player has to give the name of a creature which lives in that environment (e.g. "Whale" for Sea) <u>before</u> the Actor counts to 10. If that player can't, she/he changes places with the Actor.

5 The name of a different creature should be given each time.

Note: If the Actor counts too quickly, leader should be the one to count to 10. Leader should see that each player in circle has a turn.

MUSICAL CHAIRS
with or without the music!
(large number)

1 Place chairs in a row, with alternate chairs facing the opposite way. There should be one chair less than the number of players (e.g. 16 chairs for 17 players).

2 When the music starts, each player walks past the chairs. When the music stops, players scramble to get a seat.

3 Player without a seat drops out, and a chair is removed.

4 The player who sits on the last chair is the winner.

Variations:

1 Music may come from someone playing an instrument, or someone stopping and starting a tape-recorder using the 'Pause' button. Alternatively, someone could clap, hum or whistle a tune, stopping and starting at random.

2 For a quick end to game, remove more than one chair at a time.

THE PARSON'S CAT
(groups of 4-6)

1   Players sit in a circle and take it in turn to think of an adjective to describe the Parson's cat – in alphabetical order.

2   For example: 1st player says, "The Parson's cat is an <u>angry</u> cat"; the 2nd player says, "The Parson's cat is a <u>big</u> cat"; the 3rd player, "The Parson's cat is a <u>clever</u> cat"; and so on.

3   Anyone who can't think of an adjective within the leader's count of 5 drops out.

4   Game ends when all players have been eliminated. Last one in is the winner.

Note: This game is best played with a small number. With a large number, players can become bored if there's a long wait for their turn.

PASS IT ALONG
(10-15 players)

1 Players sit in a close circle, with one of them in the middle with eyes closed.

2 Players are given an object which they pass around (something small which can be hidden in one's hands – e.g. a cotton reel).

3 As the object is being passed around leader counts briskly to 5.

4 Player in the middle then opens his/her eyes and guesses who has the object. If right, she/he changes places with that player. (Players should have hands folded in laps when the one in the middle 'wakes' to outwit him/her.)

5 Game should last about 5 minutes or until interest flags!

Variation: A party-time game is 'Pass the Parcel' where a prize (maybe a chocolate bar) is wrapped in a number of different layers of newspaper. The parcel is passed around the circle while music is played. When the music stops, whoever is holding the parcel takes off a layer (or two) until the music starts again. The player who removes the last layer has the prize!

TEAM GAMES

are most suited to the over-7s who are learning to work for a group rather than themselves. As the urge to win is strong, it may be easy to cheat in the excitement of the game – or by intent! A leader can help children develop a sense of fair play and self-discipline by

(1) a trial run or short demo by one player so that all know the rules;

(2) a disciplined start and finish (e.g. "Straight lines" to begin and end a game);

(3) not allowing any team which breaks the rules to win.

With younger children the competitive element can be removed by not having winners – i.e.

(1) have just one team if numbers are small (8 players or under);

(2) for larger numbers, have another, interesting activity that each team can do once they finish the game.

Games in this section are written up for indoors but some may also be played outdoors.

TAG RELAY

(large number)

1   Teams line up behind a starting point:

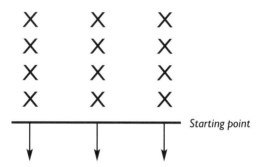

Starting point

Wall of room

2   When the leader says 'GO', first player runs up to the opposite wall, touches it and runs back to team, tapping the outstretched hand of the next player who repeats the run.
3   (Meanwhile, first player moves to the back of the team, and the others move up to the starting point.)
4   Relay continues until each player has had a turn.
5   First team to finish is the winner.
Note: If numbers are uneven, player(s) run twice.

PEG RELAY
(large number)

Materials: Container of clothes pegs for each team.

Part 1:

1 Teams line up behind a starting point with container in front of each team:

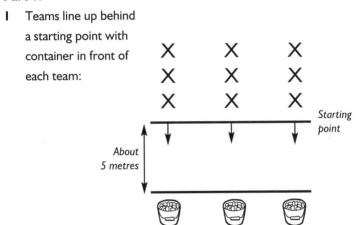

Starting point

About 5 metres

2 First player in team runs to container, takes a peg, runs back to team and taps the second player on his/her outstretched hand.

3 Second player then runs up to container for another peg.

4 (Meanwhile, first player goes to the back of team, while the others move up to the starting point for their turn.)

5 First team to finish wins.

Part 2:

Another race to return pegs to container. Again, first team to finish wins.

HOPPITY HOP

(Two or more teams. Independent scorer.)

1   Teams line up behind a starting point and face each other.

2   Players number off from <u>opposite</u> ends:

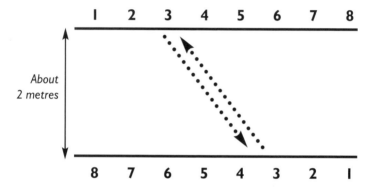

3   When the leader calls out a number, players with that number (e.g. No.3) hop towards each other and change places. First to reach new place gains a point. (If player puts foot down, she/he has to return to original place and start again.)

4   Team with most points wins.

Note: For younger children (under 7), fix the starting points closer together as hopping is not a skill usually mastered at an early age.

Try to limit number in team to 7 or 8 so that each player has a turn without the game lasting too long.

SWEET SHOP
(Independent scorer)

1 Players pair off and decide what sweet they will be (for instance, Mars Bar, Smarties). Each pair should be a different sweet.

2 Pairs form two teams and sit down opposite each other, across a wide aisle:

3 Leader calls out a sweet (e.g. 'Smarties'). Players who've chosen that sweet run up the aisle, around their team, and back to their places. First one 'home' gets a point.

4 Game continues until each player has had at least one turn.

5 Team with the most points is the winner.

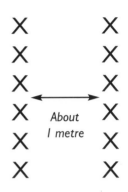

About 1 metre

Variations: Different kinds of shop (e.g. Fruit Shop).

Note: Best if numbers are limited to 10 pairs.

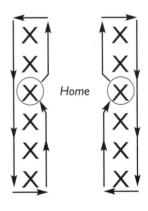

Home

DRESS THE MODEL

Materials: Bag of clothes for each team. Items could be hats, scarves, ties, large jumpers, belts, old curtains.

Part 1:

1   Leader chooses a Model for each team.

2   Teams line up behind a starting point, with their Model standing in front of them next to a bag of clothes:

3   First player in team runs up to their Model and puts one item of clothing on him/her. Player then runs back to team, taps the second player's outstretched hand, and goes to the back of the team.

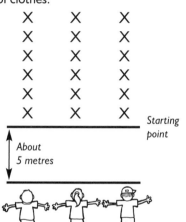

4   Second player repeats the action, and the relay continues till everyone has had a turn.

5   First team to finish is the winner.

Part 2:

1   Another race to undress the Model, when players take it in turn to remove one item of clothing and return it to the bag before running back to their team.

2   Again, first team to finish wins.

Note: Best played on a cold day or in a cold hall seeing that Models are fully clothed before the game begins!

NO SPEAKA DA LINGO!

(8-10 players per team)

Players imagine that they're in a foreign country and can't speak the language but have to mime.

1   Two teams line up with their backs to each other so that neither team can see what the other is doing.

2   First player in line runs out to face the rest of his/her team and mimes an action (e.g. swimming, playing football, reading).

3   Team try to guess the action. If they are wrong, the mimer shakes head and continues miming. If they are right, mimer nods and goes to the end of the line.

About 2 metres

4   The next player has a turn and mimes a <u>different</u> action.

5   Game continues until everyone has had a turn.

6   First team to finish is the winner.

Note: For very large numbers, more than two teams compete. If numbers are uneven, player(s) have more than one turn.

COLOUR RELAY

(Any number of teams, plus a scorer)

1 Teams line up behind a starting point and number off (1, 2, 3, etc.):

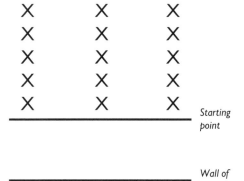

Starting point

Wall of room

2 Leader gives each member of team a colour – No.1 may be Green, No.2 Yellow, and so on.

3 Leader calls out an item with a specific colour (e.g. 'Butter'). Players whose colour is Yellow (No.2) run to the end of the room, touch the wall and run back to their places. First one home wins a point.

4 Team with the most points wins the game.

Note: If numbers are uneven, player(s) are given more than one colour.

BALL RELAY
(6-8 players per team)

Materials: A soft ball per team.

1 Decide whether ball is to be thrown over-arm or under-arm.

2 Teams line up behind a fixed point, the shortest at the front. The Starter, with ball, faces team:

3 Starter throws ball to first member of team who returns it and squats down.

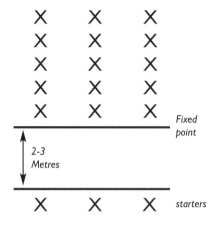

4 Starter then throws ball to each team member, in turn, who returns it and squats down. When Starter has caught the ball from the last team member, that team wins.

Variation: To lengthen the game: last member of team, after catching the ball, changes places with the Starter who becomes the first person in the line. Game continues till everyone has had a turn at being the Starter.

Note: A tennis ball would suit most children over 8 yrs.

For younger children, a bigger ball is easier to catch, thrown under-arm.

KANGAROO HOP

(teams of 5-6)

Materials: A tennis ball per team.

I   Each team lines up behind a chair:

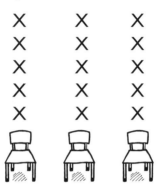

2   First player in team is given a tennis ball. She/he grips it between his/her feet, hops around the chair and back to the next player who has moved up to the chair.

3   First player hands the ball to the second player who repeats the Kangaroo Hop.

4   (Meanwhile, first player goes to the back of team, while the others move up to the chair.)

5   First team to finish wins.

Note: This game is likely to suit the over-7s, as the footwork is difficult for younger children.

OUTDOOR GAMES/ACTIVITIES

Outdoor play has the obvious benefit of fresh air and exercise and is a welcome change for children living in flats or built-up areas, especially if there is a park to play in.

Leaders' responsibility, however, tends to increase outdoors because it is harder to keep children in sight; thus, well-defined boundaries are needed.

Leaders also need to check for hazards (e.g. dog-fouling, broken glass). Such a check could be turned into a game if both leaders and children do a 'Hunt for Hazards' a few minutes before play begins.

The games and activities listed in this section are clearly not the only ones to be played outdoors. Some of the Chasing, Circle, Team and Singing Games also lend themselves to an outdoor setting. Conversely, some of the games may be played indoors.

HOPSCOTCH
(small groups or singles)

Materials: Chalk to draw the scotch on a hard surface, or a stick for an earth surface or stretch of wet sand on a beach. A flat stone, or piece of tile, that slides easily.

When the game is first played the leader should draw the scotch (right) and demonstrate the different moves.

The following instructions might be used to explain the rules:

3	**4**
2	**5**
1	**6**

1　Slide the stone into square 1. Hop in behind it, on one foot, and push it with your foot into square 2. (Try to do this without losing your balance and without the stone, or your foot, touching a line.)

2　Continue in the same way to squares 3, 4, 5 and 6. When you reach square 6, nudge the stone out of the scotch, and jump out.

3　If you can go through all the squares without getting the stone on a line, or standing on a line, or losing your balance, you've won a game.

4　If you haven't been successful, remove the stone and let another player have a turn, then try again.

Variation: Aeroplane Scotch (p.35)

AEROPLANE SCOTCH

Draw the following scotch:

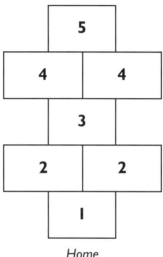

Home

1 Slide the stone from Home up to square 5.
2 Hop into square 1 on one foot, then into squares 2 on both feet, then into square 3 on one foot, then into squares 4 on both feet, then into square 5 on one foot.
3 Pick up the stone and hop around on one foot to face Home.
4 Hop back in the same way till you're Home.
5 Like ordinary Hopscotch, if you go through all the squares without getting your foot or the stone on a line, and keep your balance, you've won a game. If not, let another player have a turn, then try again!

DONKEY

(6 to 8 players)

Materials: Tennis ball or other soft ball. (A bigger ball for children under age 7.)

1   Players stand in line, with the Starter facing them with the ball.

2   Starter throws ball to each player, in turn, who catches it and throws it back to the Starter. If anyone misses a catch, she/he is called 'D'.

3   Next player to miss a catch is 'O' ... and so on, till the word D-O-N-K-E-Y is spelt out.

4   Whoever is the last letter ('Y') drops out.

5   Game continues till everyone is out.

Note: Ball should be thrown under-hand as throwing and catching a ball is usually hard for the under-7s. Skill will vary after this age.

HIDE AND SEEK or MOB
(up to about 6 players)

1   Choose a place to be 'home'. (Outdoors this might be a tree,
    gate or wall-pillar. Indoors it might be a solid armchair or door.)
2   One player is the Seeker, who stands at the home base, covers
    his/her eyes and counts up to, say, 50 <u>out loud</u>.
3   Meanwhile, the others go and hide.
4   When Seeker has finished counting, she/he shouts 'Coming,
    ready or not!' and hunts for the hiders.
5   The hiders have to try and reach 'home' before being caught.
    They tap the home base and shout 'MOB'. They are then safe.
6   The first hider to be 'mobbed' by the Seeker is IT the next
    time, though everyone has to be found first.

Note: If played outdoors, set a boundary area.

FOLLOW THE LEADER

1   One player is chosen to be the Leader (or the youth leader
    running the game might start it).

2   The Leader jogs around. The others follow and copy the
    Leader's changing actions (e.g. hands upstretched, kick-ups,
    hopping).

3   After about 3 minutes another player has a turn at being the
    Leader.

QUEENIE, QUEENIE
(8 to 10 players)

Materials: Tennis ball or other soft ball. (A bigger ball for children under age 7.)

1 Players form a line, with Queenie in front with his/her back to them.

2 Queenie throws the ball over his/her shoulder. Someone catches it and hides it. All put their hands behind their backs to outwit Queenie and chant:

Queenie, Queenie, who's got the ball?
Are they big or are they small?
Are they fat or are they thin?
Are they like a rolling pin?

3 Queenie turns around to face the line and has one guess at who has the ball. If right, Queenie stays put. If wrong, Queenie changes places with the player who has the ball.

NATURE WORDS
(pairs or singles)

1   The leader gives the players a word (length and difficulty will depend on the age and/or ability of players). Alternatively, the players could suggest the word.

2   Players collect items to spell out the word, and they then lay them out on the ground. For example, if the word were 'planet', items might be:

P	L	A	N	E	T
(petal)	(leaf)	(acorn)	(nut)	(earth)	(tin)

Note: Be liberal in accepting a player's choice, provided the items are found out of doors. Imagination is the key – note 'earth' rather than 'soil' (above), for instance.

PUSS, PUSS
(5 players)

I Four players, the Mice, have 'homes' in corners of a square with one player, the Cat, in the middle:

('Homes' may be gateways in a quiet street or spots marked out in chalk.)

2 Mice taunt the Cat by calling "Puss, puss" to another player with whom they want to change places.

3 Cat counts to 20 – Mice have to run to another home before twenty or they're out.

4 As the Mice run toward their new homes, the Cat tries to touch one. If successful, that player becomes the new Cat.

Variation: Game may be played by 3 players, or increased beyond 5 players where manageable. It may also be played indoors if there's enough space.

SCAVENGER HUNT
(pairs or singles)

1   Set a boundary for scavenging (e.g. area around a hall, one special street).
2   Give players a written list of 10 things to collect (e.g. a pebble, leaf, chocolate wrapper).
3   Set a deadline (e.g. 20 minutes) for players to return with their items.
4   Let players know what the call-in signal will be (e.g. leader will give a loud shout 'Time up', or ring a bell, or blow a whistle). (Players may also return to base with their items if they beat the deadline.)
5   First back with all items is the winner (though all players' efforts should be appreciated and checked off).

Variations:

1   Players suggest a list of items for scavenging.
2   Game may be played indoors, with items hidden beforehand.
3   Any recycling facilities locally? If so, organise a litter-pick on the way to a bottle bank or a tin bank. Set a target for the whole group (e.g. 100 discarded drink cans, 20 glass bottles, in half hour). If target reached, all are winners!

Note: Game best suited to older children (about 8-11 yrs).
For younger children, give a verbal list of about 5-6 items. If played outdoors, have enough leaders to keep children within sight.

BARK RUBBINGS

(small groups or singles)

Materials: Strong piece of plain paper (A4 size or bigger) per player, masking tape, chalk.

1 Tape 4 corners of paper to a tree trunk.
2 Rub chalk across paper until it is covered. This should produce the pattern of the bark.
3 Remove paper from tree trunk and write the name of the tree, if known, on the rubbing.

Variations: Indoors, a rubbing may be made of a wall tile, coin or button, using finer paper, chalk, crayon or a soft-lead pencil.

SINGING GAMES

Most children like to sing. When actions and dance are added to the song, there's even more fun!

DUSTY BLUEBELLS

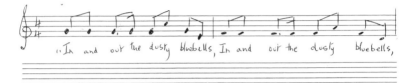

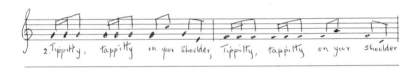

In and out the dusty bluebells,
In and out the dusty bluebells,
In and out the dusty bluebells,
Who shall be my master?

Tippitty, tappitty on your shoulder,
Tippitty, tappitty on your shoulder,
Tippitty, tappitty on your shoulder,
You shall be my master.

1   Players form a circle with plenty of space between each player.
    (Join hands, then drop them to provide space.)
2   One player is chosen to weave in and out of the 'dusty
    bluebells' while everyone sings the first verse, "In and out the
    dusty bluebells".
3   At the end of the verse the runner stops behind the nearest
    'bluebell', tapping his/her shoulders while everyone sings the
    second verse, "Tippitty tappitty ...".
4   When the second verse ends, the player whose shoulder has
    been tapped leads the way as both weave in and out. Everyone
    resumes singing "In and out ...".
5   Game continues (as above) until one 'bluebell' remains.

    Everyone then runs around the last 'bluebell' singing:
    > *Round and round the dusty bluebell,*
    > *Round and round the dusty bluebell,*
    > *Round and round the dusty bluebell,*
    > *Who shall be my master?*

    > *Tippitty tappitty on your shoulder,*
    > *Tippitty tappitty on your shoulder,*
    > *Tippitty tappitty on your shoulder,*
    > *You shall be my master.*

Note: If children wish to play the game again, the last 'bluebell'
starts it off.

THE FARMER'S IN HIS DEN

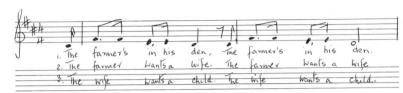

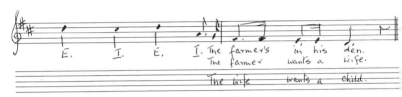

1   *The farmer's in his den,*
    The farmer's in his den,
    E I, E I,
    The farmer's in his den.

2   *The farmer wants a wife,*
    The farmer wants a wife,
    E I, E I,
    The farmer wants a wife.

3   *The wife wants a child,*
    The wife wants a child,
    E I, E I,
    The wife wants a child.

4   *The child wants a nurse,*
    The child wants a nurse,
    E I, E I,
    The child wants a nurse.

5   *The nurse wants a dog,*
       The nurse wants a dog,
       E I, E I,
       The nurse wants a dog.

6   *The dog wants a bone,*
       The dog wants a bone,
       E I, E I,
       The dog wants a bone.

7   *We all pick the bone,*⎤   picking action as all
       We all pick the bone,⎥   stop circling and walk
       E I, E I,   ⎥   towards the Bone in
       We all pick the bone ⎦   the middle.

Game:

1   Players form a big circle with the Farmer in the middle.
2   They join hands and walk around the Farmer singing verses 1
    and 2. At the end of v.2 the Farmer chooses someone to be the
    Wife, who joins the Farmer in the middle of the ring.
3   Players sing v.3, then the Wife chooses someone to be the Child,
    who also joins the others in the middle.
4   Game continues with the singing of verses 4, 5, 6 and 7. At the
    end of each verse the last one to enter the ring chooses the new
    Nurse, Dog, and so on till the Bone is chosen and the last verse
    is sung.
5   If the game is played a second time, the Bone becomes the new
    Farmer.

Variation: While the big outer circle goes around in one direction,
the ones in the middle could join hands and circle around in the
opposite direction, all singing the song.

FOUND A PEANUT

(Tune: 'Clementine')

I Players form two teams.

2 Team I starts:

> *Found a peanut, found a peanut,*
> *Found a peanut just now;*
> *Found a peanut, found a peanut,*
> *Found a peanut just now.*

3 Team 2 responds with a question:

> *Where d'you find it? Where d'you find it?*
> *Where d'you find it just now?*
> *Where d'you find it? Where d'you find it?*
> *Where d'you find it just now?*

4 Game continues with each team taking it in turn to ASK or ANSWER a question. (Allow a count of 5 for team to come up with a Q. or A.)

5 First team which fails to ASK or ANSWER is out.

6 Game may continue by teams swapping their roles of asking or answering.

NANCY AND JOHN

1. Oh Nancy, my dear will you come to the fair? The basket is read-y and so is the mare; So tie on your bonn-et and braid up your hair All on a Satur-day morn-ing.

2. I'll tie on my bonnet and braid up my hair. My new lit-tle dress I shall cer-tain-ly wear, But-ter and eggs we will sell at the fair, All on a Satur-day morn-ing.

3. Here we go, here we go off to the fair. Nancy and John up-on Dobb-in the mare Did ev-er you see a happi-er pair All on a Satur-day morn-ing.

When this game is played for the first time, introduce it with a brief discussion of (a) how a farmer travelled before the advent of the car [walked/horseback] and (b) how country people traded before the advent of the supermarket [fairs].

NANCY AND JOHN
(Pairs)

1   Players pair off and form two parallel lines about 2 metres apart. One line acts as John, the other as Nancy:

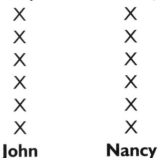

      John   **Nancy**

2   John sings the following action-song to Nancy:

> Oh Nancy, my dear, (doffs imaginary cap)
>
> will you come to the fair?
>
> The basket is ready, and so is the mare;
>
> So tie on your bonnet   (action)
>
> and braid up your hair   (action)
>
> All on a Saturday morning!

3   Nancy responds:

> I'll tie on my bonnet (action)
>
> and braid up my hair (action)
>
> My new lilac dress (holds dress in a half-curtsey)
>
> I shall certainly wear;
>
> Butter and eggs we will sell at the fair,
>
> All on a Saturday morning!

4   Both lines join <u>crossed</u> hands with their partners and gallop
around in a circle singing:

> Here we go, here we go off to the fair:
> Nancy and John upon Dobbin the mare;
> Did ever you see a happier pair
> All on a Saturday morning?

Variation: Players swap roles and play the game again.

ONE FINGER, ONE THUMB, KEEP MOVING!

Verse 1

One finger, one thumb keep mov — ing, One finger, one thumb keep mov — ing, One finger, one thumb keep mov — ing, And we'll have a jolly good time

Verse 2

One finger, one thumb, one arm keep mov — ing. One finger one thumb, one arm keep moving. One finger, one thumb, one arm keep moving and we'll have a jollygood time.

Verse 3

One finger, one thumb, one arm, one leg, keep mov — ing. One finger, one thumb, one arm, one leg, keep moving. One finger, one thumb, one arm, one leg keep moving and we'll have a jolly good time —

Verse 4

One finger, one thumb, one arm, one leg, one nod of the head, Keep mov—ing, One finger one thumb, one arm, one leg, one nod of the head, keep mov—ing. One finger one thumb, one arm, one leg, one nod of the head keep moving and we'll have a jolly good time—

Verse 5

One finger, one thumb, one arm, one leg, one nod of the head, stand up, sit down, Keep mov—ing. One finger, one thumb, one arm, one leg, one nod of the head, stand up, sit down, Keep mov—ing. One finger, one thumb, one arm, one leg, one nod of the head, stand up, sit down, Keep moving, And we'll have a jolly good time.

Verse 6

One finger, one thumb, one arm, one leg, one nod of the head, stand up, sit down, stand up, turn a-round. Keep moving. One finger, one thumb, one arm, one leg, one nod of the head, stand up, sit down, stand up, turn a-round, keep moving. One finger, one thumb, one arm, one leg, one nod of the head, stand up, sit down, stand up, turn a-round. Keep moving and we'll have a jolly good time —.

Players sit on chairs in a circle and sing the song, with actions. They add on a part of the body, and an action, with each verse.

Verse 1
I finger, I thumb, keep moving
I finger, I thumb, keep moving
I finger, I thumb, keep moving
and we'll have a jolly good time!

> poke index finger, then
> thumb, into the air,
> then close hand

Verse 2
I finger, I thumb, <u>I arm</u>, keep
moving (repeat twice)
and we'll have a jolly good time!

> ditto plus
> lift arm

Verse 3
I finger, I thumb, I arm, <u>I leg</u>,
keep moving (repeat twice)
and we'll have a jolly good time!

> ditto plus
> lift leg

Verse 4
I finger, I thumb, I arm, I leg,
<u>I nod of the head</u>, keep moving
(repeat twice)
and we'll have a jolly good time!

> ditto plus
> nod

Verse 5
I finger, I thumb, I arm, I leg,
I nod of the head, <u>stand up</u>,
<u>sit down</u>, keep moving
(repeat twice)
and we'll have a jolly good time!

> ditto plus
> stand and sit

Verse 6
I finger, I thumb, I arm, I leg,
I nod of the head, stand up,
sit down, <u>stand up</u>, <u>turn around</u>,
keep moving (repeat twice)
and we'll have a jolly good time!

> ditto plus
> other actions

> slow down and
> clap hands

HOKEY KOKEY

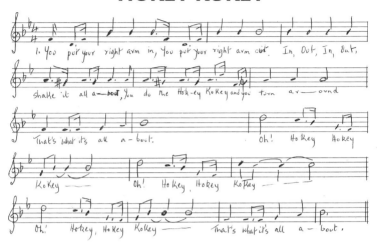

Everyone forms a big circle and sings the Hokey Kokey, doing the actions suggested by the words.

Verse 1

You put your <u>right</u> arm in,
You put your right arm out,
In, out, in, out, shake it all about;
You do the Hokey Kokey   [sway from side to side, with hands under chin]

and you turn around,
That's what it's all about!   [clap hands]

Chorus:

Oh, Hokey Hokey Kokey!   [arms up, down]
Oh, Hokey Hokey Kokey!   [arms up, down]
Oh, Hokey Hokey Kokey!   [arms up, down]
That's what it's all about!   [clap hands]

Verse 2

You put your <u>left arm</u> in,

You put your left arm out,

In, out, in, out, shake it all about!

You do the Hokey Kokey … etc.

Chorus

Verse 3

You put your <u>right foot</u> in,

You put your right foot out,

In, out, in, out, shake it all about;

You do the Hokey Kokey … etc.

Chorus

Verse 4

You put your <u>left foot</u> in,

You put your left foot out,

In, out, in, out, shake it all about;

You do the Hokey Kokey … etc.

Chorus

Verse 5

You put your <u>whole self</u> in,   [jump into circle]

You put your whole self out,   [jump out of circle]

In, out, in, out, shake it all about;

You do the Hokey Kokey … etc.

Chorus

ACTING GAMES

Imaginative play comes naturally to children. These games provide an opportunity for self-expression: the extroverts have a chance to channel their energies into a worthwhile activity, while shy children have the chance to gain confidence.

Leaders can encourage the players by seeing that all efforts – good or indifferent – are clapped.

While it is not necessary for players to dress up, a box of cast-off clothing (e.g. hats, scarves, shawls, ties) or household items (worn curtains, towels) can be treasure-trove for small groups for some of the games*.

NOAH'S ARK
(small or large number)

1   One player is Noah, and calls out the name of an animal (e.g. 'Elephant').
2   The others act out the animal named.
3   Noah chooses the best one, who becomes the new Noah.

Variation: Omit step 3 – leader could be Noah throughout the game, briskly changing the name of the animal to be acted.

NOAH'S DANCING ANIMALS

Materials: Recorder and cassette tape or compact disc; radio, or musical instrument.

1   Play various kinds of music – classical or pop.
2   Leader keeps naming different animals (e.g. a mouse, giraffe, frog, kitten, duck). Players dance to the music as they imagine that animal would dance.
3   Game might last c.5 minutes.

Note: Game might be introduced by Saint-Saens' "Carnival of Animals", where the players identify the animals portrayed by the music.

STATUES

1   Players line up facing the Sculptor who stands about a metre away from them.

2   The Sculptor takes hold of the right hand of each player, in turn, and pulls them out of the line, saying what kind of statue they should be (e.g. 'Be Batman'; 'Be happy'; 'Be the Prime Minister').

3   Each player 'freezes' into the statue required.

4   Sculptor chooses the best one, who becomes the next Sculptor calling out <u>different</u> kinds of statues.

Variation: Players run or dance around to recorded or live music. When music stops, players 'freeze'. Anyone who moves or wobbles is out. Last person in is the winner.

Note: Players should keep running or dancing – just jumping up and down makes 'freezing' too easy.

NURSERY RHYMES
(12-15 players)

1   Children begin by all singing or reciting several nursery rhymes that they know.

2   They then get into small groups and act out one before the whole group, who have to guess which nursery rhyme it is.

3   Each small group has a turn at acting and the audience, of course, claps each performance!

Variation: While this activity is best suited to younger children, older children might be interested if step 1 is omitted.

TV PROGRAMMES
(6-8 players)

1   One player stands in front of the others, calls out the initials of a programme (e.g. S-T) and mimes or acts out something characteristic of that programme.

2   First player to guess the programme correctly ('Star Trek') changes places with the player out front.

Note: If the same player keeps guessing correctly, the others have a turn by playing the game in strict rotation.

Variations: Pop Songs, Famous People, instead of TV programmes.

SOUND CARDS
(small groups)

Materials:

Version A Scissors, cardboard (old cereal packets OK) and pictures from magazines or newspapers.

Version B Scissors, cardboard, black marker pen.

Version A (Age 5-7)

1   Cut out pieces of cardboard about 8 cm x 5 cm.
2   Paste (or draw) a picture on each piece – something which makes a noise (e.g. DOG, TRAIN, CAR).
3   Place cards in a pack, face down.
4   Players take it in turn to take the top card from the pack, hiding the picture from the others. They make the sound of whatever is on the card.
5   When the others have guessed the sound, next player has a turn.

Version B (Age 8-up)

1   As above.
2   Print one word on each piece of card.
3, 4, 5. As above.

WHAT'S MY JOB?
(small groups)

Materials: Scissors, pieces of paper or card c.8 cm x 5 cm.

1   Briefly discuss jobs that people do, and practise miming one or
    two of them.
2   Players form groups of six.
3   Each player is given a piece of paper, or card, with a job written
    on it (e.g. COOK, TEACHER, CARPENTER), which players
    don't show to anyone else.
4   Each player mimes the job to the group, who guess what it is.
5   When the job is guessed correctly, next player has a turn.
6   First group to finish wins.

Variations:

1   Players think of jobs themselves. If the game has already been
    played once at the meeting, all jobs should be new ones.
2   Use pictures, not words, on cards for those who haven't learnt
    to read or have difficulty reading.

DOWN ON THE FARM
(small or large number)

1   Players sit on the floor in front of the leader who is the story-
     teller.
2   Each player is given the role of a farm animal and of imitating
     the sound it makes e.g. cockerel ('cock-a-doodle-doo'); sheep
     ('baa'); cow ('moo').
3   Be sure that each player has a role, but if there's a large
     number, players could double up (2 cows, not 1, for instance).
4   The leader tells a simple story, bringing in all the animals in turn.
     Each time an animal is mentioned, its sound is made by its role-
     model.
5   The leader should write out the story beforehand if she/he isn't
     good at ad-libbing!

IN THE NEWS
(small groups)

Materials: Newspapers (tabloids and broadsheets). Large safety pins or anything that can be used to join papers together (e.g. masking tape).

1   Choose an event, festival or theme (e.g. the Olympic Games, Christmas, school holidays).
2   Players make costumes out of the newspapers and dress up in them over their ordinary clothes.
3   Players act out the chosen event or have a costume parade.

Variation:

1   Give each group a card on which is printed the name and flag of a country. Group keeps this a secret.
2   Players use newspapers to either dress up or make an object to illustrate that country.
3   Players parade costume/s or show the object.
4   The others guess what country or object it is.

CHARADES
(small groups)

Groups choose a word which can be divided into syllables (e.g. 'mid-night'). They keep the word a secret while planning how to act out a separate scene for each syllable, then a final scene containing the whole word.

Example of how the word 'midnight' might be acted out:

1   One player tells audience that a 2-syllable word has been chosen.

2   **Scene 1** (syllable 'mid')
    Carol-singers on the village green singing a few carols, including "In the bleak <u>mid</u>-winter".

3   **Scene 2** (syllable 'night')
    The rescue of someone lost on a mountainside for a <u>night</u>.

4   **Scene 3** (whole word 'midnight')
    A <u>midnight</u> feast at a summer camp or boarding school.

Note: Players make up their own dialogue and should see that each syllable comes out clearly. However, the dialogue should be varied so that the audience is kept guessing!

Variation: Each group is given a special word, or a choice of words, to act out.

CEREMONIES
(small or large number)

Important private or public events often start or end with a ceremony – e.g. simply singing 'Happy Birthday' to someone or, on a grand scale, the official opening or closing of the Olympic Games. Players can make up their own ceremonies for special events, and act them out.

Some suggestions:
- Presentation of a trophy
- Passing an examination
- Leaving primary school for high school
- Winning a prize
- Celebrating a patron saint's day*.

* Important dates:
1 March St. David, Wales
17 March St. Patrick, Ireland
23 April St. George, England
30 November St. Andrew, Scotland

CONCERTS
(large or small number)

1   Players provide items for their own show, e.g

- singing
- reciting
- telling jokes, riddles
- playing a musical instrument
  (If one isn't available, how about a comb and paper? – SEE below*)
- tap-dancing or disco-dancing to a tape, CD, etc.
- impersonations (animals, famous people, etc.).

2   A stage might be an open space in front of the audience, or something to stand on such as a low chair or thick books (e.g. Telephone Book, Yellow Pages).

Note: If children are too young or shy to participate, they could be part of the audience who, of course, clap or cheer every item!

*Comb and Paper:

An ordinary comb, slotted into a piece of thin paper, may be 'played' like a mouth organ:

Simply blow and hum any tune through the covered comb.

QUIET GAMES

After very energetic games children are ready to 'wind down' and enjoy something which usually requires mental effort. Thus quiet games induce a calm atmosphere for a time when children need to be attentive, or have refreshments, or before going home from a meeting.

ALPHABET GAME

(singles, pairs or small groups)

Materials: Black marker pen and cardboard (blank back of cereal packets, etc. ideal).

I   Divide cardboard into 25 mm squares and write a letter of the alphabet in each square, with about 3 extra squares for vowels a, e, i, o, u.

a	b	c	d	e	f	g	h	i	j	k
l	m	n	o	p	q	r	s	t	u	v
w	x	y	z	a	a	a	e	e	e	i
i	i	o	o	o	u	u	u	a	e	i

2   Cut up into squares. Make sufficient alphabet sets for the number of players – I set is usually enough for about 3 players.

3   Players make as many words as they can from the letters in their set.

Variations:

I   Ask players to make as many words as they can on a theme (e.g. Easter).

2   Older players could make their own alphabet sets for use in the club or at home.

NAMES
(small groups)

Materials: Pencil and paper for each player.

1   Leader chooses a letter of the alphabet. (Avoid Q U X Y Z!)
    Leader, or players, choose a category (e.g. Boys, Girls, Cars,
    Fruit, Flowers, Towns, TV programmes, and so on.) Players
    write down all the names they can think of in the chosen
    category beginning with the given letter.

2   Set a time limit – say, 3 minutes.

3   Checking: Each player reads out list of names. If the others have
    any name called out, they cross it off their lists.

4   Go on to next letter of alphabet, in the same or a new category.

5   Winner is the one with the highest total at the end of the game,
    which may go on as long as wished, OR there needn't be a
    winner – just a count of how many different names the group
    can think of.

Note: Be liberal in accepting names (especially boys' and girls'
names). Best if players are roughly the same age/ability. Younger
players may be given extra time (e.g. start writing a minute before
the others) or have an older person to write down their whispered
names.

FUNNY PEOPLE
(pairs or fours)

Materials: Pencil and paper for each player.

1 Fold paper in half, then in half again, and open up.
2 Draw a head and neck on second space, keeping it a secret. Fold down to cover drawing and pass on to next player.
3 Draw a body on next space. Fold over to cover and pass on.
4 Draw legs and feet on next space. Fold over and pass on.
5 Open up the piece of paper handed to you and enjoy the artwork!
6 Give the Funny Person a funny name and write it on the blank, first section of paper.

WHAT'S ON THE TRAY?
(small or large number)

Materials: Tray, small items, cloth; pencil and paper for each player.

1 Place about 20 small things on a tray and cover with a cloth. Items might include a comb, egg cup, apple, tennis ball, a coin, and so on.

2 Check that players have pencil and paper at the ready – to be used only when the leader says 'GO'.

3 Place tray on table or floor where it can be seen by everyone. Remove cloth for one minute, then cover the tray again and take it away as the shapes of the objects can be a give-away.

4 After the leader says 'GO', players are given 3 minutes to write down all the things they can remember.

5 Player with the most correct items is the winner.

Note: A game for older, literate players. With younger children the game could be a sharing rather than a competitive experience, where children <u>tell</u> the leader(s) all the items they can remember.

BOXES

(pairs or small groups)

Materials: Pencil and paper (squared or plain).

I Mark out dots on paper – as many as you wish:

2 Take it in turn to join up dots to make boxes. You may draw
   only one line at a time EXCEPT where you see a 3-sided join ⌐
   In that case you may add a line to make a box. Claim it by
   putting your initial inside. If you complete a box, keep going
   until you run out of 3-sided joins.

3 A game in progress might look like this:

4 When all the dots have been joined up, player with the most
   boxes is the winner.

I SPY
(small number)

1   First player says, "I spy with my little eye something beginning with _____" (gives a letter of the alphabet, e.g. C).
2   Whoever guesses the right object has the next turn.

Variations: Game may be played indoors, outdoors, or while travelling. Special objects may be looked for according to the location – e.g.

Indoors:	Curtains, carpet, items of furniture.
Outdoors:	Birds, flowers, dogs, signs of the season.
Travelling:	Cars, traffic signs, licence plates.

SNAP

(two or more)

Materials: Playing cards OR pictures from magazines pasted onto cardboard. Must be duplicates.

1   Players sit around a table or in a circle on the floor.
2   The starter (Player No.1) has the pack in one hand, cards face down so that no-one can see what will be dealt out. She/he turns up one card after another, making a pile.
3   As soon as two matching cards come up (e.g. two fives or two with the same picture), the first one to call out 'SNAP' takes all the cards in the pile. (This includes Player No.1.)
4   The game continues until all the cards have been dealt out. The winner is the one with the most pairs.

THE GIANT'S TREASURE
(small or large number)

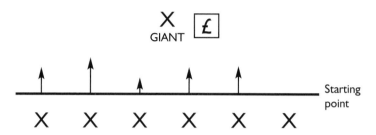

I Players sit at one end of the room behind a starting point. Giant sits at the other end, eyes closed, with back towards the others, guarding the treasure at his side (anything that is easy to pick up).

2 Leader points to one player, who creeps up and tries to take away the Giant's treasure.

3 If the Giant hears anything, he points in the direction of the sound but doesn't turn around to look. If the sound has not been made by the one creeping up, the leader says 'No' and that player continues creeping up.

4 If the leader says 'Yes', player sits down where she/he is.

5 Whoever takes the treasure away becomes the new Giant.

Note: For a quick end to a game, leader points to <u>everyone</u> to creep up on the Giant. First one to take the treasure away is the winner.

CONSTANTINOPLE
(small or large number)

Materials: Pencil and paper for each player. (The back of junk mail, where blank, is ideal.)

I   Print 'CONSTANTINOPLE' on blackboard or card or paper and display where it is easily seen. (Masking tape doesn't damage walls.)

2   Players write out as many words as they can from the letters in 'Constantinople' (e.g. in, tin, none, pale).

Variation: Any long, or shorter, word may be used (according to age/ability of players), or names/words specific to different groups (e.g. 'BADEN-POWELL' in Boy Scouts; 'CHRISTIANITY' in church groups).

Note: This game may be used as a competition among individuals or small groups, or as a shared, educational game where all the words are read out.

HOME-MADE JIGSAWS

(pairs, small groups or singles)

Materials: Scissors.

For Picture Jigsaws: firm, glossy paper (old magazines, calendars or junk mail).

For Word Jigsaws: cardboard (blank back of cereal packets or suchlike OK) and marker pen.

Picture Jigsaws:

I   Cut pictures into fairly large-sized pieces:

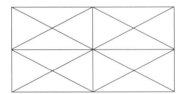 

2   Place pieces in an envelope with a duplicate picture pasted on the front. (For older or more able players, omit picture and treat as a 'blind' jigsaw.)

3   Make one jigsaw for every 2-3 players.

Word Jigsaws:

I   Print something on cardboard (e.g. a short poem) and cut into pieces.

2   Place pieces in an envelope marked with the theme of the jigsaw (or leave envelope blank for a 'blind' jigsaw).

3   Provide one jigsaw for every 2-3 players.

Examples of word jigsaws before they are cut into pieces:

(a) For a Cub Scout group

> ### Birthdays
>
> The founder of the Boy Scouts and Girl Guides, Lord Robert Baden-Powell, and his wife Olave, both had the same birthday: 22nd February. The Girl Guides call this date 'Thinking Day' because they think about the World Guide Family.

(b) For a church group

> ### Psalm 117
>
> Praise the Lord all nations!
> Praise him, all peoples!
> His love for us is strong and
> his faithfulness is eternal.
> Praise the Lord!
>
> (The Good News Bible)

Note: The picture jigsaws are likely to be more suited to the younger players. Size of jigsaw pieces, plus theme, will depend on level of difficulty desired. Jigsaws could be made by either the leader(s) or the older players for the benefit of the club or youth group.

MEMORY
(small groups or singles)

Materials: Pack of playing cards OR pictures pasted on pieces of cardboard OR words printed on cards. (Must be duplicates.)

1   Spread the cards out on a table or other flat surface, face down.

2   The first player turns over 2 cards at a time, so that they can be seen by everyone. If the 2 cards match, the player keeps them and has another turn.

3   The player continues until she/he turns up 2 cards that don't match; she/he puts them back in the same spot, face down.

4   Other players then have a turn (as above).

5   When there are no cards left on the table the player with the most pairs is the winner.

Variations:

1   Game may be played as mix-and-match, on different topics. For instance:

- The match could be between a biblical character + a book of the Bible (e.g. ADAM matched with GENESIS).
- The match could be between country + capital city.
- The match could be between languages (e.g. Welsh words/phrases + the English translation).

2   To promote learning and involvement, the players could help make the cards to be used.

WHERE'S MY OTHER HALF?
(small or large number)

Materials: Drawings or pictures of easily recognised animals, objects or people from old magazines or newspapers. Scissors.

1   Cut up large pictures into halves (e.g. if chosen category is ANIMALS*, one half could be a cat, the other half a kitten).
2   Place halves around the room in easy-to-reach places.
3   Give each player a number of halves of pictures.
4   They have to find the matching pieces.
5   Winner is the player with the highest number of complete pictures.

Note: This game could be played just for fun (under age 7), OR the one who finishes first is the winner (age 8-11).

*Other categories might be FOOD (cornflakes/milk); SPORT (bat/ball); MUSIC (drum/drum-sticks); PEOPLE - historical, contemporary or both (e.g. Queen Elizabeth II on one half, the Duke of Edinburgh on the other).

HUNT THE THIMBLE
(small number of players)

1   One player (No.1) hides a thimble in the room – where it can still be seen! – while the others close their eyes.

2   Player No.1 picks someone to try and find the thimble.

3   If the hunter goes nowhere near the thimble, Player No.1 says "Cold", "Freezing", etc.

4   As the hunter gets nearer the thimble, Player No.1 says, "Warm", "Warmer", "Boiling", etc.

5   When the hunter finds the thimble, she/he becomes the next one to hide it.

Variations:

1   Use 3 large coins or buttons instead of a thimble, telling player(s) the number of items to be found.

2   As a special treat have a 'Hunt the Sweets' or 'Hunt the Easter Eggs': hide wrapped sweets, or small eggs, in fairly obvious places in the room. Finders = keepers, but only one turn each!

CREATIVE ACTIVITIES

The accent here is on innovation, where children can find enjoyment and amusement in sharing their mental or artistic talents – and maybe surprise themselves and their leaders at the same time!

LIMERICKS

(small or large number)

A limerick is a 5-line humorous verse. The 1st, 2nd and 5th lines rhyme, and are longer than the 3rd and 4th lines which also rhyme – e.g.

> There was a young lady of Hyger
> Who smiled as she rode on a tiger;
> They returned from the ride
> With the lady inside
> And the smile on the face of the tiger!

1 Here are some limericks to complete:

– There once was a hero called Bong ...

– There was an old kanga called Roo ...

– There was a bright kid from New York ...

– A beetle got stuck in plum jam ...

2 Players make up their own limericks and share them with others.

(Limericks may be verbal or written.)

DOT ART
(small or large number)

Materials: Paper and pencil.

1   Make lots of dots anywhere on a piece of paper.
2   Now see how many different patterns you can make by joining up the dots.

Here's one example:

Variations:

1   Make dots with your eyes closed.
2   Use coloured pencils or crayons to join up the dots.
3   Colour in the different shapes.

ACROSTICS
(small groups, pairs or singles)

Materials: Blackboard, whiteboard, or poster (masking tape doesn't mark walls). Pencil and paper for each player.

1   A single-type acrostic, where the first letter in each line forms a word when read downwards, can create interest and learning. For instance, the word 'Conservation' may be used to promote care of the environment.

2   Write the word on the blackboard, whiteboard or display as a poster:

CONSERVATION means

C are
O f
N ature   –
S
E
R
V
A
T   –
I n
O ur
N ation

---

3   Players write down the acrostic and fill in the blank spaces with appropriate words. (These might be: Sea, Earth, Rivers, Valleys, Air, Trees, but all sensible answers should be accepted.)

Variations

I   For a quick game, or where players have difficulty reading and writing, let them tell leader(s) appropriate words to fill the spaces.

2   Leaders can think of numerous applications of acrostics according to children's age/interests.

3   The older or more able children could provide partly-blank acrostics (as above) for the group, together with their own answers.

KNOCK, KNOCK!
(pairs or small groups)

1   Each player takes it in turn to say, "Knock, knock!"
2   Others ask, "Who's there?"
3   First player gives a name – e.g. "Billyboil."
4   Others ask, "Billyboil who?"
5   First player gives a smart answer based on the name: e.g. "Billy boil the kettle".

More examples

–   "Knock, knock!"
    "Who's there?"
    "Egbert."
    "Egbert who?"
    "Egg but no bacon!"

–   "Knock, knock!"
    "Who's there?"
    "Isabel."
    "Isabel who?"
    "Is a bell needed on a bike?"

–   "Knock, knock!"
    "Who's there?"
    "Dishes."
    "Dishes who?"
    "Dishes the BBC News!"

WORD SQUARES
(small groups or singles)

If you look at the following example you'll notice that the words are the same both down and across:

M	I	S	S
I	D	L	E
S	L	O	W
S	E	W	N

The challenge is to create a Square choosing your own words.
Don't worry if you don't finish it in one go – you can always come back to it!

Variations:

1   Increase the size of the Square.

2   Make the words relate to a theme.

GOOD NEWS, BAD NEWS
(small groups)

1 One player begins a story with "The good news is …"

2 The next player follows with "But the bad news is …"

3 Game continues, alternating between Good News and Bad News. Those who hesitate or repeat what another player has said are out. Each addition should be in keeping with the theme. Last player in wins the game.

Example:

First player:	"The good news is that I've won a prize in a quiz."
Next player:	"But the bad news is that the prize is a bike and I've got one already."
Next player:	"The good news is that there's a car-boot sale next Saturday and I can sell it."
Next player:	"But the bad news is that I'll be on holiday then."
	etc. … etc.

MAKING UP STORIES
(small groups, pairs or singles)

1 Each group (3-4 players) is EITHER given 3 words (e.g. BOY, LAMB, LORRY) OR chooses 3 words.
2 Working together, the group makes up a story which includes these words (about 5 minutes).
3 If the group is part of a larger gathering, one member tells the story to the bigger group.

Variations:

1 **Playing cards:** Separate Kings, Queens and Jacks from the Number cards. Place in 2 piles, face down. Players pick 1 card from Pictures pile and 2 cards from Numbers pile, and use these as the basis for a story.
2 **Lucky Dip:** Each player writes 1 or 2 words on a piece of card and puts it into a container. Players, in turn, dip in for 2 cards and make up a story.
3 **Pictures:** Provide a small pile of pictures cut out from old magazines or newspapers. (Choose pictures with not much detail.) Players take it in turn to pick a picture and make up a story about it.
4 **Quickies:** Provide a bag of small objects (e.g. a coin, bottle top, leaf or piece of string). Players pick out an item and tell a story about the object for 1 minute.

PAPER PATTERNS

(small groups or singles)

Materials: Junk mail, scissors or 2-hole punch. (If no scissors handy, tear paper.)

1   Fold a piece of paper in half, then in half again.

2   Snip corners and cut a half-moon on centre fold:

Open up and you'll have a pattern like this:

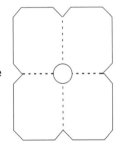

3   Experiment by making more folds and by cutting different shapes in other pieces of paper.

4   Patterns could be used as place-mats underneath ornaments and other things.

Variation: If you fold the paper (as above) and use a 2-hole punch instead of cutting out, you'd have a pattern like this:

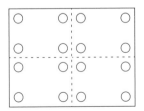

HOME-MADE JEWELLERY
(small groups or singles)

Materials: Choose from:
- assorted buttons removed from old clothes;
- scraps of coloured ribbon, wool, shoe-laces or string;
- old curtain rings (small or large, metal or wooden);
- small decorations saved from birthday or Christmas cakes;
- large safety-pins or tie-pins;
- circles of cardboard saved from the inside of jar-tops (e.g. coffee jars); coloured card saved from various sources (e.g. junk mail, old 'phone book covers);
- darning needle or thin hair-clip;
- paste

Jewellery: All kinds of adornments may be made from the above and used for dressing up in the Acting Games or dressing up for fun. Here are some items – the reader will think of others!

- **Necklace:** Thread coloured buttons onto a piece of coloured wool or string.
- **Bracelet:** Use a large curtain ring. EITHER wind or blanket-stitch coloured wool around it OR tie on bits and pieces (e.g. buttons) as a decoration.

- **Pendant:** Use a circle of cardboard from a jar-top OR cut out a diamond shape from cardboard. EITHER colour it with crayon/texta-pen OR glue a button or scrap of cloth onto it. Next, EITHER glue the cardboard piece onto a length of ribbon, string or a shoe-lace OR punch a hole near the 'top' and thread it on.

- **Brooch:** Cut out an attractive shape from cardboard and decorate it (SEE Pendant) OR blanket-stitch a small curtain ring with coloured wool. Fix cardboard shape or curtain ring to a large safety-pin or tie-pin.

Variation: Younger children whose manipulative skills aren't well-developed may like to try threading popcorn or pieces of marshmallow onto a shoelace, with the lace serving the dual purpose of needle and thread.

MIXED BAG

Some fun things don't fit easily into categories but are too good to leave out! Here's a few.

BEETLES
(pairs)

Materials: Pencil for each player. Piece of paper and dice to be shared by a pair.

1   Idea is to draw a Beetle, bit by bit.

2   To start drawing you need to throw the dice and come up with No.1 for the Body.

3   After drawing the body keep throwing the dice, in turn, to add other parts:

No.2 = head

No.3 = an eye

No.4 = an antenna

No.5 = tail

No.6 = a leg

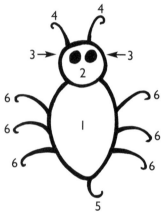

4   The winner is the first to complete the bug and shout out "Beetle!"

Variation: May be played in groups of four, players sharing the same piece of paper. As soon as a pair complete the drawing they call out "Beetle" and move to another group. First pair to get to the last group is the winner.

MUSICAL NUMBERS
(large number of players)

Materials: Recorder and cassette tape or compact disc; radio, or musical instrument. (If no music available, leader could sing, hum a tune, clap hands, blow a whistle or ring a bell.)

1   Start the music. Everyone walks around in a circle.
2   When music stops, leader calls out a number.
3   Players form groups of that number (e.g. groups of 3).
4   Any player not in a group drops out.
5   Game ends when there are only 2 people left, who are joint winners.

TARGET PRACTICE
(twos, threes or singles)

Materials: Tennis ball, container (e.g. cardboard box, empty bin) OR point marked in chalk on yard.

1 Players stand about 2 metres away from the container or marked area, and take turns at tossing the ball at the target.
2 When they score five out of five, they move back another 2 metres from target.
3 Players keep throwing, and moving back, the more they succeed and need a new challenge.

Note: For more than 3 players, have more than one ball and container or marked area. Vary size of ball/container to suit age/ability of players.

FUN WITH BALLOONS
(2 or 4 players)

1 Here's a game of volley-ball for two. The net could be a piece of string or a long belt tied between two chairs. Players tap the balloon to one another over the net.
2 Players try doubles, with four players.

Variations:

1 Players form a circle and hit the balloon to the player opposite.
2 Players have fun just tapping the balloon in the air!

WHO'LL BE 'IT'?
(small groups)

Often games need someone to start them off. Where there's a large number of players the leader picks someone, to save time. With smaller numbers (3-4), the players can work out the starter by using a rhyme to eliminate people. Whoever remains is 'IT'. Here is an example:

Tic, tac, toe

1   Players form a semi-circle, putting one hand out in front of them.

2   One player stands in front of them and chants:

> Tic, tac, toe,
> Here we go;
> Where I'll land
> I do not know.

The rhyme-chanter taps the outstretched hand of everyone, in turn, <u>on each word</u>. The one whose hand is tapped on the last word of the rhyme drops out.

3   Step 2 is repeated until only one player is left, who starts the game.

One potato, two potato

1   As in "Tic, tac, toe", players hold their hands out in front of them, but they clench their fists to act as 'potatoes'.

2   The rhyme-chanter also makes a fist, saying:

> One potato, two potato
>
> Three potato, four,
>
> Five potato, six potato,
>
> Seven potato, more.

3   Repeat the rest of step 2, and step 3 (as in "Tic, tac, toe") until only one player is left, who starts the game.

PASTIMES FOR I PLAYER

Sometimes there's no-one to play with, but a number of the activities in this book are OK for one:

There may be others that you can adapt. Have fun!

Acknowledgments

I would like to reiterate my thanks to all who supported my Millennium Project, mentioned in the Foreword, which resulted in the publication of *Games and Activities for Children age 5-11 years* (2001). Their names are listed in the first edition.

My thanks also to those who participated directly in the project. Firstly, the groups who took part in games workshops: in Dunvant, the Rainbow Guides, Brownies, Beavers, Cub Scouts, the Gospel Hall Junior Youth; in Swansea the Townhill Thursday Club and the Christchurch Primary School and its after-school club. Secondly, those who gave of their expertise at the write-up stage of the book: Winifred James who wrote the musical notation for the singing games; Bill Riseborough who provided the notation for 'Clementine'; and Robert Verdon who read the original draft and made many suggestions for improvement.

Finally, my thanks to the Millennium Commission for the Award which funded the publication of the first edition, and to the Commission's staff in Swansea and London who supported me throughout the project.

Index

AA	= All Ages: 5-11 years
I	= Infants: usually 5-7 years
J	= Juniors: usually 8-11 years